For Flora, Ron and Elaine
~J.S.

For Glen P.
~T.W.

ISBN 0-590-12691-1

Text copyright © 1996 by Julie Sykes.
Illustrations copyright © 1996 by Tim Warnes.
All rights reserved. Published by Scholastic Inc., 555 Broadway, New York,
NY 10012, by arrangement with Little Tiger Press.

SCHOLASTIC and associated logos are trademarks and/or registered
trademarks of Scholastic Inc.

12 11 10 9 8 7 6 5 4 3 2 1   7 8 9/9 0 1 2/0

Printed in the U.S.A.   08
First Scholastic printing, October 1997

I don't want to go to bed!

by Julie Sykes

Pictures by Tim Warnes

SCHOLASTIC INC.
New York Toronto London Auckland Sydney

Little Tiger did not like going to bed.
Every night when Mommy Tiger said,
"Bedtime!"
Little Tiger would say,
"But I don't *want* to go to bed!"

Little Tiger wouldn't let Mommy Tiger clean his face
and paws, and he wouldn't listen to his bedtime story.
One night Mommy Tiger lost her temper.
When Little Tiger said, "I don't want to go to bed!"
Mommy Tiger roared,
"ALL RIGHT THEN, YOU CAN STAY UP ALL NIGHT!"

Little Tiger couldn't believe his good luck.
He scampered off into the jungle before
Mommy Tiger could change her mind.

Little Tiger went to visit his
best friend, Little Lion.
When he arrived,
Little Lion was having
his ears washed.

"It's bedtime," growled Daddy Lion.
"Why are you still up?"
"I don't want to go to bed!" said Little Tiger,
and he skipped off into the jungle
before Daddy Lion could wash
his ears, too!

Little Tiger decided to visit his second best friend,
Little Hippo.
He found him splashing in the river,
having a bedtime bath.

"It's bedtime," bellowed Daddy Hippo.
"Why are you still up?"
"I don't want to go to bed!" said Little Tiger,
and he scurried off into the jungle before
Daddy Hippo could give him a bath, too!

Little Elephant was Little Tiger's third best friend.

He went to visit him next.

Little Elephant was not out playing.

He was in bed, listening to his bedtime story.

"It's bedtime," trumpeted Mommy Elephant.

"Why are you still up?"

"I don't want to go to bed!" said Little Tiger,

and he bounced off into the jungle before

Mommy Elephant could put him to bed, too!

Little Tiger thought he
would go and find
Little Monkey,
his fourth best friend.
But he found Mommy
Monkey first. She put a finger
to her lips and whispered,
"Little Monkey is fast asleep.
Why are you still up?"

"I don't want to go to bed!"
Little Tiger whispered back.
Quickly he tiptoed into the
jungle before Mommy Monkey
made him fall asleep, too!

Little Tiger didn't know where to go next. It was the
first time he had been in the jungle so late by himself.
Even the sun had gone to bed!
Suddenly it seemed very dark.
What was that?

Little Tiger looked up
and saw . . .

. . . two very large yellow eyes
staring back at him!

The eyes belonged to a bush baby.
"Shouldn't you be in bed?" she asked.
"I don't want to go to bed,"
said Little Tiger
bravely. "*You* haven't!"
"That's because I go to
bed when the sun rises,"
said Bush Baby.

Little Tiger couldn't imagine
going to bed in the sunshine!
He shivered and thought how
cold and dark it was in
the jungle at night.

"I'm going to take you home," said Bush Baby.
"Your mommy will be worried about you."
"I don't want to go home! I don't want to go to bed!"
said Little Tiger. But he didn't want to be left alone
in the dark either.

So Little Tiger followed Bush Baby through the jungle. He was glad of her big bright eyes, showing him the way back home.

"We're almost there," said Bush Baby, as Little Tiger's steps became slower and slower.

"I don't want to go to . . ." said Little Tiger sleepily,
dragging his paws.
"Oh, there you are," said Mommy Tiger,
"just in time for bed!"

"I don't want to . . ." yawned Little Tiger,
and he fell fast asleep!
Mommy Tiger tucked him in
and turned to Bush Baby . . .

. . . but the den was empty.
Bush Baby had disappeared into
the jungle before Mommy Tiger
could tuck *her* in, too!

"I don't want to . . ." yawned Little Tiger,
and he fell fast asleep!
Mommy Tiger tucked him in
and turned to Bush Baby . . .

. . . but the den was empty.
Bush Baby had disappeared into
the jungle before Mommy Tiger
could tuck *her* in, too!